Caesar Who is a young, part-time writer, who lives in a peaceful island country, Cyprus, with three furry feline babies. Besides his passion for literature, he works as a psychotherapist who proudly helped many on their mental health. He also holds master degree diploma in psychology and specialised in sexuality.

Caesar Who

THE MISTY WALKER

Austin Macauley Publishers™
LONDON • CAMBRIDGE • NEW YORK • SHARJAH

Copyright © Caesar Who 2022

The right of Caesar Who to be identified as author of this work has been asserted by the author in accordance with section 77 and 78 of the Copyright, Designs and Patents Act 1988.

All rights reserved. No part of this publication may be reproduced, stored in a retrieval system, or transmitted in any form or by any means, electronic, mechanical, photocopying, recording, or otherwise, without the prior permission of the publishers.

Any person who commits any unauthorised act in relation to this publication may be liable to criminal prosecution and civil claims for damages.

This is a work of fiction. Names, characters, businesses, places, events, locales, and incidents are either the products of the author's imagination or used in a fictitious manner. Any resemblance to actual persons, living or dead, or actual events is purely coincidental.

A CIP catalogue record for this title is available from the British Library.

ISBN 9781398459458 (Paperback)
ISBN 9781398459465 (ePub e-book)

www.austinmacauley.com

First Published 2022
Austin Macauley Publishers Ltd®
1 Canada Square
Canary Wharf
London
E14 5AA

1

Oscar's is the best nightclub in town. For a good price, you can please your taste buds with all kinds of fancy cocktails of the secret recipe, or hook up with beautiful, just-old-enough chicks to empty your balls, or simply allow the crushingly loud music to bombard your senses and dance as if tomorrow will be Solomon Grundy's Saturday. It's my personal favourite too; every Saturday night's visit has become my routine since the day I was able to get in. The owner, Mr Oscar, even reserves a special seat in the southeast corner for me on Saturdays. The seat is comfy and with romantically dimmed light where the music reverberates the best in this area.

The best part is that I don't have to lose a fortune every time I visit this paradise of orgy, unlike everybody else. Thanks to my occupation, I rarely spend actual cash on anything. I pay people with favours.

In Oscar's case, I had earned his extra hospitality by fixing his son's problem a few years ago. Davis Oscar is a rich and infamous playboy who messes around every day with his old man's pockets. Not somebody I usually offer to help but when he got too high the other day and punched a reporter in the face, knocking out two upper teeth, Mr Oscar the paternal caregiver couldn't sit tight anymore. Money can be regained but reputation rarely recovers. So, when he returned to sanity after hearing about his son's wrongdoings, he called me. He had never called me before. I don't even know how he acquired my number but given my reputation in the problem-solving business, it'd be understandable he managed to get it from other giant figures.

I did the cost-benefit analysis swiftly and agreed to help in return for the best seat in my favourite club free of charge.

Therefore, just the next day, the poor reporter's dentist 'accidentally' pulled two more teeth out from his upper jaw. And in that private, sterilised dentistry room, I appeared. With the stench of blood and the smell of clinical alcohol haunting in the air, I leaned over and whispered to the potential accuser, "One more word added on that report you are writing, one more tooth you say goodbye to. I'm afraid you can't afford to finish that sentence."

One hour later, when the front-toothless man dashed home, that uncompleted Word document entitled 'Local Reporter

Brutally Assaulted by the Son of Entrepreneur Clark Oscar' was forever erased from his laptop.

Thus, here I sit comfortably, consuming free drinks and enjoying a VIP strip dance right in front of me.

I'm watching as well as my head wandering; they say those who can't hear the music think those who dance are crazy. I do hear it, loud and crystal clear, and when it is too loud, the pink squishy meat in my skull echoes with it. However, I still consider the dancing as crazy as the madness of Cthulhu tales. I understand the urge of moving one's torso and limbs to relish the music but ultimately, I fail to comprehend its extreme extent. I see youngsters twisting their bodies of youth and waving them to the rhythms, and at the sight of this orgy, I sense insecurities and incongruities. Young men who hope to advance their careers and raise a family, put on silly faces and adopt ridiculous dance moves to please, pathetically, a few equally young ladies around them. And these young women in peacock mini-dresses and red-bottom heels, who are supposed to live free from shackles of misogynistic social constructs, twerk their booties and flash their 'assets' to attract young men. This is all for the sake of their attention-seeking needs. And above all, they behave such incredible joy, which inevitably exposes them in the shade of their collapsing misfortunes that may emerge and crush them any second.

I'm no such joy demonstrator. That being said, though, I do indeed experience happiness. I do not celebrate the secretion of the little chemicals named dopamine in my head; I just experience such materially synthesised feelings in a minimal way and that of peripherally in a world of feasts of triumph. It's as if I were a thirsty man unable to acquire water looking at a photo of sour cherry and chilling in a physical state of salivation.

At this moment, I sip from the Stella in my palm; the golden nectar of rejoicing, waters my stone-cold heart of peace. I lay my sore back down a bit on the sofa and calmly receive the input of the sights of modern morbidity.

My shoulder is lightly tapped by a lean figure from behind. It's Clark Oscar, formally dressed, which is an aristocratic law he seldom follows. He puts on his phoney smile and yells over the strong oppression of the loud music, "Come, Mr Atticus. I need to show you someone."

We walk through a long, gothic hallway as the noise slowly fades. We progress on our short trip to a VIP room with a medieval-style door hidden in plain sight, looking like a dead end with dark red fancy wallpaper. The only reason I recognise it's a door is that it's not fully closed. Inside, I see a young man weeping and a middle-aged man raging.

Oh, I recognise the man. It's the current mayoral candidate, Mr Osman.

I follow Oscar's gesture to enter the room, and the thick door smashes closed behind me as my presence is noted by the two gentlemen inside, leaving even the nightclub owner out of this meeting.

"Mr Atticus. Greetings. Have a seat." The man gestures me to an armchair, lights a cigar smoothly, and says, "You don't know who I am but…"

"Candidate Osman, sir, it's all on the news."

"Good, so it saves some words. You may wonder about the secrecy here but you see…"

"I know what I do, Mr Osman. I can imagine."

"To do us both a favour, don't interrupt me. I came for help but still, know your place."

"I know my place well, sir. And so I know the situation here. This weeping young man is, and I presume, your son. It's his problem you need me to solve." I cut him short, turning to this 20 something and starting my routine questions. "So, drugs?"

The young adult reacts slowly, his pupils motionless and shining under the cover of his wet eyelashes. Blood-red networks of capillaries appear behind such humid curtains.

"No? Worse? Murder?"

His eyes tremble for one beat, scared by this massive word but I can tell by his wet yet motionless cheeks that's not it.

"I see. Not this bad. Sexual scandal?"

His pupils heavily shake among the red vessels on his eyes, as if a dancing star performing on red carpets, so very nightmarishly elegant. Tears start to overflow. It seems his father is quite mad about it but I can't blame the old man. This mayor-to-be could lose his career because of it.

"You raped someone?"

The young adult says nothing but his weak mentality lets his facial expressions confirm my theory. The old man's forehead wrinkles even more as if multiple Mariana Trenches had been compressed together, and dipped down to the centre of his eyebrows. He's really stressed out.

"So you've done it, Junior Osman." I turn to the older man. "You see, the way I handle business, equality between both parties must be preserved so is the trust. You came to me for help. You had no choice; I have plenty. But also you are the mayor-to-be, the man of tomorrow. I'd love for you to owe me a favour. Therefore, will I do the job, and you will tell me what I need to know and withdraw your unnecessary pride?"

"You are a dirty hired gun! If I want, I have all the evidences to put you in jail for life. You know that? Even your dirty deal made with Oscar. Yes, I'm aware. I can make your life miserable."

"Together with all those powerful people who have dealt with me? I don't think so. But I'm glad you have some leverage because, at this moment, we're equal." I try my best to not savour this moment but my lips still tilt on one side for a split second. Fortunately, he doesn't notice. "Therefore, sir, as I said, I know my place and my range of choices. Oh, I know them well, and hopefully so do you."

He silences himself then slightly nods his head.

"I understand you don't want to have anything to do with a guy like me. That's some good spirit, sir. Really. And I actually appreciate your integrity. You see, I'm not a murderer; I'm a problem solver. And there are always problems to be solved no matter how noble you are or how just you are. You know the saying, 'You either die a hero or live long enough to see yourself become a villain.' I beg to differ. You may die heroically but you can never be the hero, or rather, we are all villains because, one day, there must be one day, the shit will knock at your door, and it will storm in. The moral man has his dilemma. The trolley comes, inevitably, either one man or five men, the blood will stain him, and there's no way out."

I sort out the situation for him. "I've heard your plans for the city. You are going to make a change to this filth. That's fantastic, sir. Those new policy regulations will definitely save lives. But your son has troubles that, if exposed, will make that dickhead candidate Donald Trump win the mayoral race. So, here's your choice: make a compromise or fail the city."

The father closes his eyes hard as if a horror haunts him before his eyes. It must be a tough choice. Silence freezes the room, with only a few sobs generated from the young man and his apologies that merely worsen his father's headache. I wait for this honourable man to ponder things. I wait patiently.

I doubt whether I meant every word I had said. He's a good man, and he's going to be a good mayor. But I'm not sure if I'm happy for that, nor am I certain if I just want him begging me to help or encourage him to make a sacrificial move for the good of this city. I have dived too deep into this filthy and absurd world to even remember what kind of man I am. This sort of situation used to be a dilemma for me; help someone de-scandal for the greater good or retain my integrity to keep my hands clean. But now? I just want to work.

And I get my work. Mr Osman finally opens his eyes, sighing softly, and lets the son tell me the details.

"I wasn't...I wasn't going to do anything to her, I swear."

"I don't give a damn, boy. Here's a problem, thus, I solve it. I'm an eraser, not an equaliser." I tried to calm the boy, using my kindest voice to channel his youthful rationale. "Give me details, and details only."

"It was two weeks ago on a Friday night. Johnny and I were hanging in my apartment, a boy's night, you know. I just bought a new PlayStation 5 so all we did was play video games. And suddenly, he told me he wanted to invite his girlfriend to come over to show off some Overwatch action figures we bought. Then Anna came but with this other girl, Helen, whom I'd never seen before, too. So anyway, we hung together in my apartment, with ordered pizza and some drinks…"

"They brought drugs?"

"No, no way. I never do that, my father needs his reputation to win the campaign, and I'm always being extra good."

I peek at his old man's face, and I see a touch of pride for his boy for a second, blossoming like spring flowers but it quickly fades into the dark clouds on his face. Nevertheless, the 'good boy had just fallen' theory is confirmed.

"We had a great time but Johnny and Anna can't drink too much, so they passed out after three rounds. I kept conscious until round five, and this girl, Helen, out-drank me pretty soon."

"That's it? You can't recall anything after you were drunk?"

"I woke up on the next day around lunch, and I had no memories. Then, yesterday, we got an unsigned package at my apartment's door. It was a tape, we played it, and the video shows me doing it, with Helen." The boy's trembling slightly intensifies, and eventually evolves into a state of shaking that resembles mild Parkinson's.

"Can I see the tape?"

"They are clever; the tape burned automatically right after its play," said Mr Osman.

"She said she wanted something from you?"

"One million euros. She said she wanted me to bring the cash, alone, to the riverbank under the bridge, on Sunday morning at 4 a.m." The father leans towards me to show a piece of a note found in the package beneath the burnt tape. The words had been printed out in a common font as if it were an innocent note from a fortune cookie. Yet, it possesses the power to ruin a good mayor's career.

"OK, so this blackmailer is smart," I comment. "What exactly do you want me to do?"

"You are the damn expert." His voice is now mixed with a touch of contempt, which I don't mind. "You tell me!"

"Well, we don't know if someone is acting behind this Helen or if she intentionally seduced/drugged your son and plotted such blackmail. She might have helpers. The safest way to solve this sort of problem is to pay them what they want, always. We can't have law enforcement units helping,"– I gestured at the mayoral candidate–"Because of, you know, your reputation. Besides, given the obvious fact that whoever planned it, did it well, we must not act carelessly. The cards I usually play do not apply in this scenario. Therefore, I recommend the sacrifice of your campaign money. You are able to afford it. Money can be regained; opportunities never return to your grasp."

"I can't believe you're actually suggesting the gentlest method." He pauses a while in uncomfortable silence, then employs his sarcasm, "You, out of all people."

"Meanwhile, I'll guarantee, of course, that in two days, after you have delivered the cash, the tape you get from her will be the original and uncopied." As usual, I don't mind his application of sarcasm.

"Fine. So it is. I'll prepare the cash tomorrow." He dims the lights, and his face sinks into the shadows.

2

The greatest mayor in the history of this city may be Mr Osman, who is going to owe me a large favour. To ensure that everything must go correctly, I have to investigate some details, such as, who is this Helen and what she is up to.

So I do knock on the door of her friend Anna's apartment.

A young woman answers the door. She wears lingerie, a rosy red bra, and a matching bikini-style bottom with a pair of red lace stockings. She is not so much in her mood of shyness, on the contrary, she leans on the door, demonstrating shamelessly her tanned, skinny-fit body of youth. She also doesn't seem annoyed to be bothered in her private time. She brushes her hair to the right using her fingers that clawed with long purple nails.

"Yes, sir?" she asks.

My eyes wander around on her so-desirable body for a few moments but then lock on her face. "Anna?"

"Yes, I am. Who is asking?"

"I'm a police detective. Name's Atticus. Can I have a word with you, young lady?" I flash my badge hanging from my belt. It certainly is a counterfeit but the confidence in my words compensates for not clearly presenting my ID.

"Sure." She shows me the way in. "Something bad happen?"

"I'm actually not allowed to give any information, this is one classified issue, ma'am. Please understand, I'll just ask a few questions."

I sit myself down, watching her grab a cold drink from the fridge. Her bikini bottom fails to cover her round butt, and as she bends over for the drink in the fridge, I enjoy purely aesthetically such sight from behind her. The hip-waist ratio of golden represents her fertility, and to be frank, a man no matter how abstinent or noble, fall before the mysteriousness of 1.618. Caesar, the great, knelt before Cleopatra, was he the old general so desperately aching for a worthy successor? Or the surging billows of lustful love conquered the conqueror? The red phantom of sexiness before me calls me, like Jesus knocks the door of my heart, asking to be worshipped.

"Are you a model?" I have to ask but such curiosity comes not from Eros at all, only pure query cuts my thoughts short and into a neutral question.

"A supermodel, Mr Atticus. Victoria's Secret."

"Victoria's Secret? I thought they were bankrupt."

"Not really. They cancelled the fashion show in 2018 but still need someone like me. Or rather, some 'body' like mine." She turns over and goes a bit saucy on me while showing her tender breasts barely covered by her Wonderbra.

I remember Victoria's Secret fashion show in its glory days, and her proud words took me back to 2012 when Miranda Kerr was my then celebrity crush.

I was watching an interview regarding how these angels were supposed to, as requested by the promotion team, look fresh and shining on stage, nothing unlike supermodel Anna now, and to resemble a goddess that 'seemingly just had a perfect sex'. Yet, such a description confused me. They might look stunning and aesthetically appealing but nowhere near sexually attractive. They dressed in a few strips of cloth and/or leather, revealing their young and firm skin but those tendons in the inside of their thin thighs, uncovered by that sleepwear, look absolutely disgusting. I understand the beauty of fitness. I even appreciate some muscular figure in women (As I'm not a man with fragile masculinity) but that! And the heavily tanned skin with moisturiser (I assume) reflects the spotlight as if some dark brown metallic decoration in the 'German-style' household interior finish. It feels like a sort of ultimate objectification or perhaps reminds me of the human skin suit in the Texas chainsaw massacre's origin story.

They might look like goddesses but definitely in a screwed-up mythology! Greek goddesses, at least, are portrayed in a nicer and 'lazier' tone with the white robe sliding down slightly on their tender shoulders, bathing in the sunshine of holiness of the Olympics. While Valkyries wouldn't be so revealing, they resemble the characteristics of loyal guard dogs and fierce warrior lynxes; their starry aura of transcending spirits shining within a dark moonless sky.

If they just had some perfect sex, I'd prefer them before such transformations. Supermodels are supposed to be the most attractive creatures on earth. Yet, they disappoint me a lot.

Therefore, a mixed combination of feelings emerges within me. I lose my certainty whether this beautiful Anna before me stays a beauty or falls into an abomination.

And the bringer of such uncertainty speaks, "So, what do you want to know?"

"I have an interest in your friend, Helen. How did you know her?" I focused back on why I came and try to hide my intention and this issue that dramatically troubles young Osman.

"She's a colleague of mine, well, more or less. I mean, she's a manikin model."

"Manikin?"

"Oh, it's that kind of model who attracts attention solely by their bodies."

"And how does that differ from you?"

"Total opposite, less catwalk on the runway, more posing in the studio. Basically, I put on high-fashion wear to demonstrate the beauty of clothes' design and colouring to the audience, my body serves as no more than a hanger. But her, those clothes on her simply decorate. She's showing the world the natural gorgeousness of human flesh."

"That's…well put and sounds delicious."

"Oh, yes, mister. Don't quote me to my boyfriend but Helen is really a damn masterpiece."

Anna stares into my eyes, smirking silently and forcing on me unwanted images of Helen. Those images are sensitive enough to unease men's nerves and erotic enough to erect any man's shaft. I studied psychology in university back in my youth, more specifically, sexuality. I understand the toxicity of the sexiness of women to men, thus I'm able to have a helicopter view on such toxicity and distance myself from a situation of sexiness overload. But I flunked this very moment, not that I was physically aroused or anything but after quite a while of peacefulness, my masculine mentality encountered a road bump of unsettling thoughts. Unspeakable as it felt, both malaise and rejoicing bombarded my mind, not for something sexual but overwhelmingly intimate. As when a lady does not want sexual intercourse right away, she requests her husband to cuddle. Or rather, like a stableman sees a Ferghana horse galloping on the boundless field, stretching its beautifully grown muscles, the horse-keeper's mind would be intrigued like falling in love, his dopamine would secret like pouring but such passionate affection involves not a single touch of lustful filthiness.

Now I'm the mad appreciator of Anna's non-sexual sexiness.

I look away from her line of sight and notice myself slightly blushing, swallowing saliva. "I'm assuming you're close?"

"Very much."

"Did she appear to you abnormal recently?"

"Not really. Why? She's unwell?"

"I believe she will be fine, that's what I can tell you." I figure that mentioning Osman will be a bad idea. Stealth is one of the main features for men doing my job. "She got a boyfriend?"

"Yes, name's Andreas."

"OK, if you are so kind, can you tell me where I can find them?"

"Sure."

She writes down the address again revealing her cleavage.

However, I do not savour such a view, the address she just wrote down marks the exact abandoned half-built building next to my house.

How unfortunate is her trick's result…sneaky, cunning, but unfortunate. And how dare she? After all that sauciness before? I feel betrayed. And my fury intensifies as my vision locks on her tan-lined breasts. Such beauty shamelessly tricked me and lied straight at my face? This non-conformity fuels my rage.

Yet, I still manage to hide my emotions. I'm a black belt in such capability.

"Oh, by the way, I hope you understand the importance of not informing Helen about my arrival?" I pause between my words to make the vibes scary while keeping direct eye contact with those two pretty green rings around her pupils. It's a useful trick, and it works perfectly each and every time. "Or I'll have to do something." I lie back in the chair, exposing the black hard weaponry of offensiveness that is tucked in my belt while my right fist tightens as it rests on the sofa, showing the abusive power of mine over hers.

"Or you'll have to what? You will kill me, Mr Atticus?" She giggles; in the innocence of such words and such laughter, there's less flirting or taunting showing because I can tell that from one trace of uneasiness in her voice.

I have gained leverage, for that she's scared.

I patiently wait for the even weirder and tenser atmosphere emerging from the silence and for the tidal heat retreating from my cheeks. I slowly return to my devil mode. The saucy flirting earlier was fun but slightly too uncomfortably intimate for me. However, the discomfort seems advantageous at this very moment. The human mind is designed to drop our guard when the air turns sexual, of course, such a habit applies to other positive affections as well. Thus, I use such programming of brain responsiveness in my favour.

The room is warm but her nipples harden even under the thick cover of the Wonderbra. She sits straight and lowers her drink down on the table, crossing her long stockinged legs and folding her arms. Around her chest, these folded slim-but-fit arms levitate her tender breasts, with the further facilitation of her Wonderbra, those two beautifully rounded half-spheres climb up just below her collarbones. She's becoming defensive, considering the current situation of her presence. We stare at each other. Her green eyes go a bit watery but her pupils barely dilate. She needs another push.

"Keep guessing; it will be your scariest guess."

She might be hiding something from me because of the suspicious non-necessity of the flirting with me earlier. Well, I guess I'm very aware of my limited attractiveness for a supermodel like Anna; she is definitely out of my league. She made me uncomfortable, now it is my turn.

"Is that a threat?" Her voice does not soften that much but her toughness gives her away. Such a rhetorical question is supposed to be offensive but that hurtling panic in her eyes speaks otherwise. She has entered the fight-or-flight mode.

"No, dear, not at all. You see, when I asked if you noticed anything abnormal about Helen, you asked back if Helen's unwell. You used your concerns for her to distract our conversation. It may seem sweet and innocent but is it? So, no, it's not a threat, it's a kind reminder if you forgot anything.

"You seduced me with your body but thankfully, I was immune. Then you seduced me with the idea of Helen. If I'm being honest, it worked a bit. But now here we are. I'm the cold-blooded reptile, calm and ruthless, and you are the little mammal, hot but harmless. Therefore, I suggest you try again to answer my question, what's up with Helen?"

It takes a while but then she says softly, "She was in a melancholy mood recently, like for real. Yesterday I went to her place, her real place but I only found Helen crying and Andreas furious. I thought they'd had a fight but when I offered a hug to comfort her, she pushed me away saying that she wanted nobody to touch her again."

"She never said that to you before? Even when she was depressed?"

"Never. We models have this narcissistic obsession with our bodies. Our confidence in body image and the willingness to show it off are what we're making a living from. Nudity and appropriate physical closeness are daily routines for us. She never said it before so I know she must be hurt. Badly."

I take a glance at her stance, scared and helpless, sitting in an armchair. She even grabs a feathered overcoat to cover her skinny curves in this fairly warm room. Her eyes are humid, and her tears blink in her eye sockets like a miniature starry sky, showing only, a deep concern for Helen. This may be the sign of true telling.

I can't deduce a conclusion based on these limited leads. As a man doing what I do, I should be clearing out a bloody path, if necessary, for my client. But as an empath, I can't help but sympathise with these youngsters. What a bright future they have. What a gift of beauty they possess, all trivial before the crushing tragedy of some old men's power game. Either it's blackmail, as Osman said, or he lied about his monstrous act, I just have pity for all at this moment, the moment not of truth but of silence.

"I will find out what exactly happened, and I'll be fair," I say to the weeping girl, "I promise."

"Will you? Don't you have to do what you must? Whatever that is?"

"This is different. We men punch each other in the face, kick crotches, even stab deep and send them to ICU as if we play the damn house. But there is a line on hurting women, physically or mentally. Women are the creatures of holiness, the creation of purity, and no man may contaminate her majesty. As amoral as I am, free of the shackles of the stupid common laws, I have integrity, which means courtesy, honesty, and chivalry."

"Alright then. Thank you." She is convinced by my speech. I always have such a gift of persuasion but this time, I just spoke from my heart.

"Now, is there anything else you noticed about Helen so that I can help?"

"Oh, I saw an opened suitcase in her bedroom. She must be packing."

"Was it a large suitcase? Had she packed a lot?"

"No, it was a tiny one, like for a one-day trip, two days tops."

3

I don't lunch in town as I am supposed to. I have to rush to Mistyhill, the only suburban county within a half-day drive from the city. How likely was Helen going on a pleasure trip randomly to nowhere like Mistyhill? Nothing made sense. I need to know what she's plotting and hunt down her possible conspiracy.

The clock is ticking. I have only a little time to find out what Helen is doing in Mistyhill. The day was Friday; the sun has sunk, and the hour hand is pacing near the number six.

My vehicle is unfortunately anchored a few meters before the tiny billboard on the highway, reading "Welcome to Mistyhill"! On this pathetically small and unnoticeable billboard, there is a sight of horror that doesn't catch my attention at first but when it does, it haunts me, and I know will haunt me for the rest of my life. The last three letters and exclamation mark should be painted neon green like the other letters are in blood red. The very first moment my glance rests on it, I think the green paint has faded for some reason, as the bright colour of other letters is a bit age-worn as well. But the reality shocks me. The reddishness of these four lean characters is not due to the years of weathering but to four dead bodies of sheep; hanged, headless, limbless, gutted, and completely skinned, like four goddamn scarlet totems.

I don't vomit, despite the sight. Perhaps the wind of late autumn has chased away its smell but I am shocked to the core. I tell myself to calm down.

I grew up on my grandpa's farm. I've seen worse.

I've indeed seen worse but the worst is yet to come. My childhood memories about that farm are triggered as if Satan's demonic subjects have opened the ground and crawled up from what's beneath my feet. Animals, those dead sheep and those rabbits, with their distinct and traumatising, disgusting smell, step closer in my mind. Not that I don't like animals and nature but something within me is itching.

My feet grow sore, and I realise I have been standing still in the middle of an empty highway for five minutes straight, totally motionless. The vibe in the air repels me, like a magnet of the same pole. I am not welcome. I look over the mountains that stand afar. Sitting among them, the town centre of Mistyhill bathes in a sunset glow as the quiet, vacant, and dead night mist creeps forward. I suppose no one was welcome.

I direct a phone call to a friend of mine in an intelligence agency. "Michael, do me a favour. Check the county named Mistyhill. What happened to it in the past 30 years? I need to know why this place is so damn creepy that even the welcoming billboard literally reeks of death. I swear to you, there are four dead skinned sheep hanging on it."

He must be assuming I'm exaggerating but the truth is that my words are completely literal as anyone in my shoes can tell. Anyway, I keep my trip going but now on foot.

Along with the narrow street down this hill, the mist that had spread in town is slowing my approach. The white milkiness comes up and eventually, cages me as I finally reach the foot of the mountain. The town unveils itself, yet not a single figure of shadow appears in my sight. I am the only stray. So, I follow my instinct to wander into town.

I can tell the presence of local inhabitants in the neighbouring residential buildings. Household lights pierce through their windows and illuminate the pebbled road under my feet. It's 10 p.m. but no pedestrians show themselves in the streets. I wonder if there's some sort of curfew.

The mist grows heavier; this small town becomes even quieter. These short buildings standing beside me seem to slouch as if melting in steam, emitting a vibe of unspeakably

With my somatic being absorbing heat, and my mental being pondering over the haunting strangeness of this puny, creepy town, my phone rang. It was my friend Michael. "Hello? Michael? You find anything?"

"Yes, there was an unreported document regarding this Mistyhill about 20 years ago. A local cult called 'Absentees' committed a mass suicide of 54 deaths but no media reported that tragedy as much as it deserved. Only a few journals described it, and they certainly did not catch people's attention for some reason. I'm not sure. Here it says…"

"Says what, Michael?" I step out of the lobby, ensuring nobody will eavesdrop.

"There is this police report that says the leadership of this cult, who also killed themselves, were Zed and his spouse Leda. They inspired many of their fellow dwellers in Mistyhill to commit suicide in the grand church of Mistyhill and later conformed."

"Geez, say it again? The grand church? In town centre?"

"Eh, let me see." Michael pauses but his voice soon returns. "Yes, town centre. How do you know?"

"Never mind, can you find the name Helen in this story? She seems important here."

"Ah, I can find a pending police report that has been pending for 14 years. Eh, governmental departments, right?"

"…"

"It was a complaint against the police deputy chief, Mr Osman, for his 'false accusation' of the two cult leaders. It says Osman had slandered them for being responsible for the mass suicide. It also claims that the two were also victims of such an evil movement and that Osman accused them as great villains were unforgivably unprofessional and too vicious to not to be sentenced to death."

"Osman, the mayoral candidate?"

"Yes. And this report was filed by the girl you were asking about, Helen."

4

When the sun rises to its peak and its light of blessings finally eliminates all remaining mist in the streets, I fix my car along with the leftover chill in my spine and the ache in my lower back. I drive down the highway and head directly to the town centre.

The four bloody-red totems of terror hanging on the billboard kept watching me while I was fixing my ride. Perhaps this explains why I sweated even more than a morning of hard work would cause. I dared not look up but my disobedient mind kept checking them out. Such slaughter and terrible display must be the doings of the cult, ruthless and tasteless. I wonder what deity they worship and, most important, how much Helen is involved. Because, I have to admit, I hold pity for this young lady growing up parentless. In such an already miserable childhood, she must have suffered greatly from the blame of being the daughter of 'devils'. I can't tell if her accusation of Osman's is just but I can feel the fury and pain of a young and lonely girl.

The steering wheel in my hand starts to get slippery; my hands are sweating. My stomach feels funny too as I keep visualising poor Helen. She must be beautiful and have a desirable figure, men go crazy wherever she goes but in the years of hopeless solitude and her parentless existence, nightmares must have haunted her. Did she grow up in an orphanage? Did peers bully her for the alleged sins of her parents? Did the blame drown her like a pool of murky water and swallow her whole? Did she project her miseries on the former police officer Osman? Was that all the blackmail was about? Revenge?

More important, is she going to return the original tape? Driving my car, I feel like my body is being torn apart from the middle, or as if I were having twins and the two babies that I give nutrients and care to are crawling sideways and ripping me open. My masculine mentality wants to protect her and shelter this poor little girl against all harm. I tell myself that my existence has been lucky for not experiencing such sufferings, and I can never fully commiserate with her. My empathy shakes me to the core.

I even spent last night picturing, figuratively, the wounds on her delicate soul, to the extent that I can't help but even envision our marriage and my care and love melting her ice-cold wounded heart. I hold her white lace-gloved hands while speaking my dearest vows out of my heart in the rain of Sakura petals and promising that I'll never let her down or give her up. I whisper the words of comfort softly into her ear when we share a king-size bed. Also, when we are hanging on the streets, my arm stops her careless marching into a busy road, and I walk in front of her showing the way with the loveliest worry in my eyes. Not knowing much, my one-sided dedication to saving her from what I imagined is her pain, has only exploded.

However, she is wanted by my client, and I'm a man with my professional ethics. Because, without a career, the axioms of social constructs will define me no more. Besides, with my poor experience in getting along romantically with ladies, perhaps this complex of reverse Stockholm syndrome has escalated too quickly.

I've arrived. I stare out the car window at looming gothic architecture gradually enlarging itself at the end of the stretch of suburban road. It's truly a beauty in a cultish sense with pale vertical spikes piercing midst-humid air, an aged bulky main structure standing still in rough winds showing signs of centuries of mist. It denies this giant's shine, yet its vibrant gravitas had not shed even one bit. It's hard to imagine that this elegant creepiness indeed exists in the wasteland of Mistyhill but the fact shut me up. Thus, I park and enter.

The decoration and furnishing style resembles those of Christianity; statues of various saints stand peacefully at the sides of the hallway with marble structure and golden details. There are no haloes levitating above their heads, and there are no animated expressions at all, their faces rest, calmly looking down in prayer. At this time of day, there aren't many attendees. A few elders sit in random seats, whispering; their rustle softly echoes in the vastness of the church. In the front of the pews, where there should be hanging the grand cross in Christianity's tradition, there is nothing at all. It is a roomful of empty space bathed in darkness. No lights seem even to dare to bother the dimness, and the air, along with candle's flame that barely lights up the chapel, slightly trembles before everybody, jumping and blinking as if a blurry sight of a starry sky, calm and viciously charming.

This is unexpected; a cult usually revolves around personal worshipping for, of course, personal benefits but besides the weird vibe in the air, I sense nothing morally unjust. Everything here looks like a normal minor religion of monotheism for a less developed county.

And certainly, there are no signs of Helen.

I look around again, equipped with my manhunt radar but eventually, it is fruitless. I approach a monkish-looking young man for information. I explain to him my status as a visitor as well as my willingness to learn a little about their religion.

"May our lord hear your interest, sir. Although our worship usually preaches not, I still have the pride to share my lord with you. What is it you'd like to learn?"

"Ehh, first of all, who are you praying to? Who's your Lord?"

"Our Lord is no mortal, neither is he immortal. He is beyond time and space; he birthed such continuum and fathered fate himself. He is the absence of all; he is the nothingness, the void."

I stare back at the darkness in the windowless space at the front of the chapel and go speechless. It's the first time in my knowledge that a cult would worship an anti-being. Besides amazement, I picked up the word 'absence'. Is this the cult to which Michael is referring? Are they the murderers who caused 54 casualties including Helen's parents? I start to plot how to ask about the poor girl; perhaps I need to pretend to be a curious outsider a bit further.

The monk closes his eyes and whispers:

"A priest who preaches not, a worshipper who prays not, and a monk who solitudes not.

A sun which shines not, a father who disciplines not, and a deity who does not.

Spinoza believed in nature. I worship the very opposite, the absence of nature.

Plato assumed the logos. I devote to the opposite, the absence of ideals.

Freud manifested libido. I demonstrate the opposite, the absence of life drives."

I ask him, "Then what do you do? And what do you have, if all of your essences are absent?"

"Look at these people." He points at the tiny crowd in their seats. "They are not praying; they are nothing like all others. They just come to church and slowly march toward inevitable death in peace. We do nothing in the name of our Lord, yet we do everything. The actionless action is what we do, and the beingless being is what we have."

"It seems pretty minimal to me, almost suicidal," I say calmly while my eyes lock on him, implying the crime they committed decades ago that ruined Helen's childhood.

"Perhaps, Mr Foreigner. But death is just a relief, more like a blessing; it corrects the original sin and the fundamental mistake of mankind of being born. We might be suicidal, as you assumed but to die is not the point at all. Rather it's to reach the balance before the last exhalation. We end only when our debts are paid and credits are refunded. Nothing unlike the Egyptian myth that tells the story of an afterlife: The soul-taker Anubis would value the weight of your heart with a piece of feather on his balance. We too have our algorithm for such a moral valuation process. For example, in our belief, the death penalty is much more lenient than imprisonment. Such ceasing to exist serves no punishment for anyone, therefore, we judge and sentence sinners by our legal system as if to play the traditional sense of God himself, humbly."

I am amazed by his speech, and my curiosity is triggered. I give a pause to my tricky questions. "Alright, then how do you punish someone that traditionally is thought to need to be put down if the death penalty is too lenient?"

"It would depend on the exact criminal act he committed. If he kills, we make him suffer until he begs for death, if he rapes, we publicly rape him, if he caused panic, we make him even more afraid. For example, we believe in the traumatising effect of mental torture. If there's an anti-depressant, we can create 'depressant', if there's a tranquilliser, we can invent a 'paniciser'."

"That sounds very controversial. It's not your job to decide who's guilty in this life, neither is it to punish people so harshly. Why do you have to do that?"

"The Lord didn't set the rules or the penalties; he set us to fulfil the order of the universe upon the chaos of men. Even if you disagree with our religion." He stares right at my eyes and says to me, surely and seriously, "At least understand that there has got be someone to do it. If not us, who? If not so just, how?"

"What happened to the actionless action? Beingless being? What happened to your stoic mentality and the calm spirituality? Where came all this rage and fury? If I were a clinical psychologist, I'd have sessions of cognitive behavioural therapy with you for at least five years!

"Does your unwillingness to preach originate from the toxicity of your ideas?" I ask.

"Say whatever pleases you. We don't preach because our religion is not for all people; it's too individualistic. But we have applied such laws for centuries; the world isn't ready for such divinity, yet in this town, we had achieved greatness. The people here, though only a few, are law-abiding, moral, and ethical. We literally build a paradise out of the mist!

We found our meaning, in our Lord's name, from our 'harsh' laws, from our lifetime of balance of order and chaos, and give and take crime and punishment!" The young monk's eyes are shining in passion and enthusiasm, like the fireworks on national days but never for one single second do I sense anything right in his vision.

"Do you people ever tire? Of this? At least?"

"What do you mean?" he asks.

"'Rising, streetcar, four hours in the office or the factory, meal, streetcar, four hours of work, meal, sleep, and Monday, Tuesday, Wednesday, Thursday, Friday, and Saturday according to the same rhythm. And you find meaning? Such life, or rather, any life in this world is simply tiresome, unfulfilling, and meaningless. Even just the mere thought of it, and my mind starts numbing, dying, and decomposing. We are but some boring unity of stardust trapped in the form of a quickly decaying body in a hopeless money-hungry society on a dying planet with forests of steel in a mysterious and absurd dimension. And you spent all your pathetically worthless lives on punishing people with scary pills?

"Your nihilism on life does not falsify my belief."

"No but it falsifies your enthusiasm. I spent my puny life fulfilling deals and contracts of sorts, and it swings forward and backwards like a pendulum between boredom and suffering. But at least, I was calm. When I bore, I know my life is worth living because of its mediocrity, when I suffer, I feel alive with the knowledge of my self-awareness. I don't care, at this point in this stupid conversation of ours, if your laws were just but you are too passionate, and that is your sin."

"Anyway, I did not come only to judge your religion. Besides all, I kinda wish to see how exactly effective your legal system is."

"Oh, it's extremely effective," he assures me. "We don't just invent drugs of different kinds to mentally punish offenders; we are also specialised in recreating a scenario that induces different emotions." He leans over and proudly whispers, "Just this month, we have prepared the real inferno for a sinner, and you will never imagine what that's like. Maybe you had heard of this story of Mistyhill 20 years ago, the mass suicide? This man incriminated our holy ritual and framed us for being a cult; he caused infamy and pain to our town and now's the payback time."

"Wait, what did you say?"

I am so shocked, my senses fail to register that a bulky figure emerges suddenly behind me and strangles my neck with full force. Shortly, my voice is muted, and my head goes spinning.

He yells at the monk, "How is he here? This is Osman! Didn't you recognise him?"

"I...I didn't know, he just showed himself in the chapel, I thought he was just some tourist!"

"Fine." The shadow behind then turns to me, "Mr Osman, you are early! Can't wait for your hell? Helen sent her greetings to you!"

He elbows me at the back of my head. I don't lose consciousness but my knees can't hold my weight anymore. I finally collapse. I can feel that he drags me back to a corner and throws me into a pit. I fall down into darkness, unable to see anything.

After a while, I pick up my sanity, and that is when I realise my situation is totally screwed up. The uneven floor of this basement dungeon sends its chill into my body. I reach out my hands to sense it, only to gain an answer of horror. The floor is piled up with bones, human bones perhaps. I dare not to presume conclusively its true nature. The bones are wet but feel meatless; perhaps they have been lying here for ages. I encourage myself to explore more about my surroundings by crawling around. Shortly, my knees and palms are aching intensely because of the spiky bones and pointy teeth.

There is a complete absence of light; only the ache in my eyes is projecting black shapes and uneasiness onto my irises. I almost blackout from the bombardment of the smell of rotten flesh, just after the return of my olfactory sense. Such sensational horror hurts my stomach deeply and profoundly, and I reach the limit of my tolerance. I try my best to keep the contents in my belly right where they belong, yet my vivid imagination is no help at all. I gradually visualise, without any input of lights or images, such a dark hell that consists of mountains of human bones and whatever kind of rotten flesh that is haunting this dungeon.

5

This abyss of darkness does not stare at me. It swallows me whole.

The smell of rotten flesh reminds me of those four diabolical scarlet totems of death hanging on the highway billboard. I had hope of closing this case, and with confidence in this manhunt, I was holding true feelings for this girl, Helen. Yet here I am, locked alone in a dark dungeon with nothing but human bones and rotten flesh.

My mind, under such a situation of despair, wanders into my memories.

Short-term memory: My fixed car was waiting for me outside of this gothic church, not far upstairs. And my phone had left my pocket during the strangulation. So, I am supposed to dash back to the city to warn Osman about this dungeon and people's hatred against him but now that I finally found out her motive, I lose my way back home.

Long-term memory: The surroundings remind me of my childhood, not that I used to live in hell but the smell of death resembles that of my grandpa's farm. There were sheep there too, bloodily slaughtered or pathetically put down if sick. I remembered my early days on that big old farm of my grandfather's.

I was at the naïve age of 12, and I was living with him on his farm. He was one grumpy, weird elder. Despite being highly educated, he did nothing in his long life but scold and roughly raise my father, who eventually couldn't stomach such a bad, strange temper and left the household when he was old enough. This was an irony because even though my old man knew how terrible my grandpa's parenting was, he still left me with Grandpa for the first 14 years of my childhood. I was lost in the pursuit of the exact reasons for my old man's uncaring decision for me but perhaps, in the name of some untraceable sentiments, he meant good for me. Maybe he agreed, despite being unwilling to admit it, with grandpa's method of bringing up a child.

Just after my 12th birthday, my grandpa told me that he had to travel to some overseas farm to import a few new breeds of lamb. And because of the early death of my grandma, there would be nobody else to look after me, except the owner of a neighbouring farm, who happened to be Grandpa's friend. So I was sent to him, Earl the piggy farmer, for three weeks.

The first week went surprisingly well. Earl was nice to me, and so was his granddaughter Lizzie. She was around my age, young and innocent, with an immature mind and undeveloped body but her smile became one of the few reasons I woke up in the morning. She was slightly shorter than me, which was indeed short because I wasn't tall either. She had two big watery eyes that melted my heart instantly at any time she cast her sight upon mine. She had also beautifully trimmed bangs and a shoulder-length ponytail, which even today I can remember bouncing when she skipped, just like the tails of those little piglets running around in her farm.

She was my first love; uncontaminated love in an amazingly free summer at the age of 12.

I was a premature boy, before I grew into a grey ace, I had feelings down there, and I had fantasies since 11. I started to touch myself to explore more, and I had nameless dreams that were slightly sexually charged. I dreamt about older girls who appeared in the magazines and how they would kiss my young lips and my underdeveloped pecs. I dreamt about their skinny curves posted on the coloured pages of magazines and how these sexy women would miraculously be attracted to a silly boy like me. Yet in every dream that Lizzie was involved in, my fantasies went more romantic and less 'passionate'. She held a place in my heart nowhere like those sexy ladies. At that age, I'd crave an intimate night with them but I'd crave more for just a ten-minute walk around the farm holding pinkies with Lizzie. At that age, I'd fantasise on lonely nights of licking all over a hot chicks' body, each and every inch of her skin, not yet for sexual foreplay, just for the chemistry. But I'd fantasise more about putting my head against Lizzie's just to feel the warmth through her bangs on my forehead to experience the puppy love of purity.

At the end of three weeks, I didn't have the chance to tell her my feelings but I was somehow sure she was fully aware. She gifted me a kitty cat to say goodbye and to offer, perhaps, her feelings back to me. I named the cat after Lizzie, and I took Liz the cat as a souvenir of my most treasured memories back to grandpa's farm.

On my way home, I can't help but tell him about Lizzie. "And we held hands! I think she definitely likes me back! I can't be sure but this is already amazing!"

"Hm."

"Grandpa? Are you happy for me?"

"Hm."

"Grandpa, how was your first love? Was she grandma?"

"Boy, there's something in this world that looks so beautiful that its beauty overwhelmed its toxicity."

"But I don't understand, Grandpa."

"It's like happiness; you rejoice your life increasingly as if climbing up the mountain but eventually you'll fall, eventually it disappoints you, it kills you. And the more you took in the joy, the harder you fall, and the bloodier your remains as you finally see the ugliness of happiness. Earl ever showed you the piggy slaughter? Those piglets had a lifetime of happiness in gluttony and sloth, and eventually, they got cut open and sliced. The fatter they grow, the longer they suffer. Boy, are you a piglet?"

I didn't understand fully at my naïve age, neither was I willing to accept any bullshit Grandpa said. I grabbed Liz the cat and showed her to Grandpa, "No way, Grandpa! There is something beautiful, and it will last forever! Like Lizzie and, just like this cat! Look at it. Isn't she beautiful? Even when she snores or when she sleeps upside down, her face is always cute and adorable!"

I thought my argument was invincible, for Liz the cat was indeed one breathtakingly beautiful feline. Her big green eyes were decorated by her razor-thin pupils under the noon sunshine, which also coated her fur with a layer of the golden aura. Her white short hair had no impurities at all, like the colour of milk of Grandpa's best lamb. She sat on my palms vigilantly as if she were a king of his frozen land covered in knee-deep snow governing his kingdom of glory.

Grandpa went furious for some reason that I wasn't able to comprehend and stopped the car immediately. He grabbed the cat away from me, took a carving knife, and ripped her open right in front of me. Her precious fur was instantly drenched squirting blood; her screams tortured my soul like the bell of doomsday, loud and unspeakably horrifying. He put her trembling body above my head. Fresh feline blood and starchy feline bodily fluids poured upon my face and all over my torso. He made another cut. Liz the cat reacted less violently as she was in dying condition but her intestines and faeces rained all over me just like her blood did before. The smell of flesh and gore shocked me to the core. I lost my sanity immediately from all the foulness showering me.

"You still think it's cute? And adorable? Boy, breathe it in and taste it, the blood, the gall, and the shit. Your little girlfriend Lizzie is the same creature of ugliness. You think she's beautiful? She is the same filth when cut open, full of shit in her belly! Open your eyes wide and see it, all the foulness, just like the damn cat!"

His words put an end to my childhood as if all other things were in vain. I don't blame him for such mental destruction. Perhaps a truth like this may only be learned the hard way, and in comparison with other harder ways, a gory shower of my Lizzie seemed trivial and unworthy of mention.

In memory of Grandpa, I finally vomit on the piles of bones but shortly adjust my churning stomach. I have a quick shiver and shake off my stress and uneasiness. I must find a way out of this dungeon.

I force myself to stand on my feet and try to jump as high as possible to hold on anywhere on the ceiling that may be grasped. The darkness is torturing my senses. My eyes have adapted into this blackout but my vision, or rather the image my brain receives from my irises, starts to become funny with silly shapes and random objects of blackness flying all over as if I am lost in the snowy mountains on a stormy day, except the snow was as dark as Vantablack.

My ability to smell is certainly disabled. The downside of not sensing the terrible scent of rotten flesh is being unable to detect any scents from upstairs, which offers no help at all at this moment of desperation. I try to yell but the sound insulation of the four walls is unexpectedly brilliant. No one, I bet, even some young worshippers with good ears, who stand a few feet right above me, can notice my presence.

"You are not Osman. He is supposed to be here tomorrow! Who are you, intruder?" The voice, like moonlight cast into such absence of brightness from above, the sound itself, almost moves me to tears.

"Of course, I'm not whoever that is. Who are you? Let me out!"

"My apologies. My men thought you were someone else. I'll fetch you up right now."

I am finally rescued, after a few hours of hellish experience. I feign ignorance, demanding, "Damn, why would you put someone there? Who are you?"

"You don't have to know, sir. I understand that you are a visitor. Now, please go back to your city before the mist puts you in lockdown." Helen speaks to me softly. I know it is she, and damn, she looks so fine.

Her lightly messy long hair sticks a little on her pale cheeks and thus beautifully decorates them; her eyes, pure and seraphic like an angel who just landed on earth, watery and clear as if a muse just wept for love; her nose is fine yet soft and pointy like a female highlander character portrayed in amine-style; her lips are bloody red, the bottom one bitten lightly by her china-white teeth while the upper one slightly tilts at the ends, looking so very kissable.

As a manikin model, she also has incredible curves, young tender bosoms swelling elegantly under the thin cover of a blouse. A slim waist emphasises her firm, round bottom, which dances with every step she 'performs' in a pair of extra-fit denim jeans. But such a performance does not seduce me because her succubus-like sexiness does not appeal. Instead of being a Mrs Robinson in *The Graduate*, it impacts me differently. I felt I went back once again to my 12-year-old self. The attraction those cover girls fed me gave me no sexual arousal but a sense of grave need for intimacy. No penetration, no fingering, even no kissing, just a hug, so that her warmth of femininity and her scent of divinity may be conducted to me through her thick bang to my frontal lobe.

I am lost in her eyes for a few minutes. I even forget to confront her about the tape and all. But upon remembering, I look around me in this chapel full of her men. It would be a bad idea to grab my pistol and point at her in front of them. I won't do that anyway. It stands against all the laws of my integrity regarding how to treat a woman, especially a young gorgeous woman; therefore, I tell myself to retreat tactically, and the reason is that the guy who knocked me out is standing right behind me at this point.

So, I flee. Without any contact method for Osman, I am driving fast on the highway, dashing back to warn him about the surprise party Helen has prepared for him.

If this cult is about retribution in an inhumane manner, that dungeon of darkness and gore is supposed to be the original suffering of Helen's childhood. Does that mean that she also spent days in the cave of insanity before being rescued? The speedometer on my ride surpasses my personal highest. I keep thinking about the case 20 years ago; men died and rotted in the cave of horror, a young girl survived her parents' madness but to spend days of solitude in hell. Loneliness, starvation, and unspeakable fear weren't easy to be processed by a child; they might destroy one's all, take away what's defining a man 'a man'. Did she cry until dehydration? Was there no more water, and just salt secreted from her eye sockets? Did she have to consume her fellow villagers' flesh? Or rats or maggots? She screamed for days only for the help that came too late? Did the silence in there surround her as if the mist in town swallowing?

And to take her revenge, Osman has to suffer the same and eventually, beg for a swift death. A good man, guilty or not for his doings, is to end his life in such a bitter way, and there's no sugar-coating at all.

Yet I am still a bit late. The clock tells me the time is 04:14, Sunday morning. I abandon my ride at the riverbank, with the door open and engine on. I see a tall figure and another bulky one interacting far away in front of me, Mr Osman and probably Helen's boyfriend Andreas. They don't notice me at all, quietly exchanging ransom and the tape in a tense atmosphere.

I yell as I run; a high pitch in a morning this early. It brings the attention of early risers who are making coffee in the residences of the next neighbourhood and thankfully, Osman's. But the moment he turns, Andreas grabs Osman from behind and drags him away into a van near him.

I can't do anything to stop him. I run back to my car, expecting a race to rescue my client but he was so very prepared. The second I jump in the car, he already has escaped my sight.

Under the bridge, a man was taken to a hell so horrible that I'd rate it a ten for its torture. I stand on the riverbank, alone, freezing, and with a suitcase full of cash that Andreas didn't even care to take away.

6

I could just walk away because, as I declared to the Osmans, I'm a contract problem solver, not an equaliser like Denzel Washington, I don't have the required skills or such commitment to handle my guns to singlehandedly clear a bloody path and save my former client, who had just been kidnapped to hell. And according to international contract law, when Osman dies, which will be the case very shortly, I have no responsibility to carry on my job. Besides, regardless of even my contractual obligations, it seems like Osman probably deserved whatever the hell had to offer. False accusations and abuses of justice, with valid evidence of such viciousness, will otherwise be waiting for him. If that's not hell, it is still imprisonment.

But young Osman needs a father; the city needs its good mayor.

I call the Osman boy to plan the next move. That winning baby was weeping like crazy over the phone but fortunately for him and his family, another much more reliable housekeeping business-managing figure does exist in his household, Victoria Osman, the firstborn. On the phone, her voice sounds placid, almost indifferent to her missing father but I can somehow tell the deep bond in their shared bloodline. Her calmness comforts the boy's nerves, even dims my worries somewhat. Her decision of a meeting between us is shortly arranged. We will see each other in the same secret room at Oscar's.

When I am at the club, I do not necessarily feel any sort of stress but waiting in my spot in Oscar's, allowing all crushingly loud music to trample all over my sense of sound, I sense a touch of extra uneasiness, something that I could not easily process, something that I swallowed wrong, and this bulge of foreign matter in my throat keeps bouncing upward and downward with my breaths. I can't tell my exact feelings towards Helen, and her cultish friends back in Mistyhill. They have their own reasons.

From a rather young age, perhaps when I was still in that farm, I learnt to dissociate from the reality and the norm of the crowd. Such distancing allowed the survival of my sense of superiority, which perhaps was the sole mental support that I had to stay sane in the tough childhood in the devil's farm. I learnt to crown myself secretly so that the harshness of reality bothered me less. I'd see all human sufferings, either mine or others, as beneath me and unnecessary to be experienced personally.

The price of such superiority, however, was that I gained a heavy amount of compassion for all my 'subjects' as human fellows. For instance, I suffer greatly in guilt, despite my doings and some small, wicked sense of achievement, for the threat that I made to the journalist boy in that dentistry room for Clark Oscar. Or, when I acted scarily and intimidating before Anna the supermodel, I felt bad. I had a flirty affair in my mind with the marvel of folksy sexiness of hers, yet I betrayed such warmth and even intimacy of common people's sexuality by souring it. I had killed the divinity of all this chemistry. And in the case of Helen, I keep stressing to myself about the necessary evil of Osman's execution and her convincing reasons behind it, regardless of how cruel it might be. What was believed as sacred and holy by the suicides was said to be cultish, what tragic and depressing departure of her parents was said to be wicked acts of the chief culprit of mass murders. In loneliness, she must have wept; the people must have mourned in a consensus of blame. She must have been wounded, the people damaged.

I don't know, in Osman's defence, how or why or under what circumstances he framed these people and Helen. Maybe he had to search for a scapegoat as the public always needs a target to hate, and it was a choice made out of no choice. Perhaps in the night of such decision, he too suffered in guilt staying up in the bath of the morning stars' lights.

To act or not to, that's the question.

The Oscar's music feels noisier in the manner of actual loudness but at the same time quieter in the sense of my subjective listening. The strippers dance even more erotically, twerking booties and opening legs widely but as usual, I feel nothing. The joy-seekers surge in their jumping with the rhythm of exciting music, as if experiencing life's highs and lows in a rapid cycle. I wait for half an hour consuming my non-alcoholic drink, and soon after emptying the fancy glass, I am, just like the last time, summoned by Oscar to the room.

The room patiently awaits. A young lady is quietly exercising her privilege of using it, sitting alone and attracting my full attention.

My realisation that the two Osman siblings are half-blooded comes soon. Victoria is an Irish lady, red hair, fair eyes, pale and heavily freckled skin. She is plain looking but seems well-educated and well-mannered. She sits straight in an armchair with her legs crossed. Her little black dress is cotton in an extremely simple design, looking somehow casual, like what Audrey Hepburn would wear on a fishing trip on a late-summer day in *Roman Holiday*. She doesn't put on heavy make-up or high heels, which suit well with her style, nude-colour lips shining dimly in soft lights, quite unlike the bloody red lips of Anna. Hers were much more approachable and 'cool', as some mansplaining guys would call them.

We shake hands and settle down to plan a rescue.

Manpower is in extreme scarcity, and we have no idea what kind of organisation we are dealing with. Is it just a criminal mastermind duo with a few followers? Or are we talking about an entire cult of members that had spread over the whole village of Mistyhill? We are able to mobilise the resources and labour originally from the campaign team, a dozen committed personnel or so, as well as the cash I retrieved from the crime scene under the bridge.

"Secrecy is the priority, we have money but we don't have the world of people to trust," she stresses.

"How many trustworthy men do you have in your campaign team?"

"Around one dozen. You need them armed?"

"It's your decision to make. Armed or not, if we go in forcibly, we are talking about a small invasion, and I don't expect they'll come along, bloodshed they had been through, bloodshed they're willing to let there be again."

"That'd be my worry. You have your speciality to avoid lawsuits and the punishing legal system; that's what you do.

On the other hand, though we may get destroyed or die eventually in prison, we have reasons to fight."

"Yes, I can withdraw from this mess anytime. But besides business, I don't wish to see you lose in this war. You said you have your reasons. I believe so. I'm a man with a loving father too. But such risky action would never be what your father wishes to happen. Think about what he would expect you to do. Campaigns can lose, old men can die. There's always a future for you and your brother."

"And leave my father in hell? I'm not a traitor bitch that turns against my own father. According to your description, that place doesn't sound like a proper nursing centre, and I will refuse to let him die and rot there. They started this war. No one in this team will rest until we rescue him."

"Well, I don't know who started it. But I know that this war will only end when either your men and your family spend the rest of your lives in jail or that entire village gets wiped out from Google Maps. How else can this end? We can negotiate with them; their religious beliefs were though cruel, rather more intellectual than just a superstitious blind stupid cult. We may have some chances to lessen Osman's pain."

"How dare you, sir? He is not dead yet! We hired you, and you are in team Osman, not that bitch Helen and her damn boyfriend!"

"Yes, I understand. But I need a reason more than just an oral contract." I have fallen into a pit of dilemmas, unable to decide. Both options are harmless to me technically, as she says. I can always withdraw myself and go with the wind, leaving all this mess behind. But it is exactly this innocuousness that gives me a hard time on determining the next move. "Give me one day, just 24 hours, if I get what I need."

"Yes?"

"We make it public. The daughter of former cult leaders has abducted a mayoral candidate. It will be a huge hit for any media channel, and if we control the consensus, I can get military help for us. There, that's what you wished."

"And the tape?"

"It will be gone as if never existed."

"Alright. 24 hours, go."

7

Michael has probably dug six feet under the archive room to find relevant documents about Helen, Osman, and the mass suicide case 20 years ago, yet what we got on our table were only a few files with some pictures.

And expectations had been met. We found absolutely nothing that might lead to the answer to my question, was Helen's revenge just?

I need an answer to ease my cognitive angst of making such decisions, to motivate me to carry on the onslaught of Mistyhill, and to comfort my guilt after all is done.

But I know I will have no answer, only my confirmed decision. What is just? A choice made out of none, and a reasonable revenge for her miserable lone heart, which side to blame? The only thing to blame, if we can, is the cruel indifferent fate of us all.

I stare at the ancient picture of bodies piled up in that dungeon. With a flashlight on at the scene, I can see their unclosed eyes reflecting brightness, like the eyes of black cats in a black night. The shininess brings me back to yesterday, and I can't help but allow a chill to creep up my spine.

Thankfully, good news interrupts my chilly panic. It was the club owner who breaks the ice, his voice mixed with a touch of excitement, and he gives me a lead. "Mr Atticus, as your request, I found a girl that came from Mistyhill! She is actually one of our working girls in Oscar's. I didn't realise that until Davis reminded me. She will join you soon in a VIP room. Enjoy!"

I didn't expect my luck in Oscar's might assist my case, and I certainly didn't expect a random search for Mistyhillians to succeed at a nightclub, given that even the documents served no help like this. I find I am glad and excited to meet this Mistyhillian escort girl.

As I walk into the VIP room, a first for me, I notice its fanciness. Unlike the secrecy of the hidden room at the end of the hallway, this room has been made for endless pleasure. Iced alcoholic beverages of sorts, a king-size bed surrounded by rose petals, space heaters sending warmth into my torso; there are even different brands of complimentary condoms sitting on the nightstand. But of course, before seeing all these sensational charms, I see a beauty, barely dressed, sitting on the bed.

"Hi, I'm Atticus. What's your name?"

"Up to you. My name is whatever you want to call me." Her words are all flirty but the tone of them possesses not a bit of dirtiness, soft voice vibrating in the warmth of the air, as if the final melody of a classical masterpiece symphony flowing endlessly in this very room, making me ache for the feast for my ears one more time.

"I'm not a client today. May I ask a few questions as a friendly chitchat? I'll pay for your time."

"...Sure, it's your call. But I'll have to warn you, there were men doing this trick, they pretended to befriend me but actually just wanted more committed sex. These innocent words won't fool me. You see, I sell my body, not my sentiments."

The word 'sex' muddles the atmosphere and my innocent intentions, even though this room is designed for this very purpose of men's carnal pleasure. For years, I always feel unsettled when I hear this word. It pierces my eardrums. I'd prefer the slang for it, fucking, which feels, though inelegant, powerful yet relaxing. Its power originates from the emotions it usually involves, and the relaxation comes from its casual usage. Another alternative is 'making love'; it's certainly more romantic, so much so that this phrase fools people into the illusion that sex itself is somehow sacred. I beg to differ.

"I'm no man like those reproductive bags of garbage, though my words may not be able to prove anything. I want to hereby promise you, I'm not a damn dog in season all year."

"Do you not want sex with me?"

"I don't want to fuck you. I want to either hold your hands and die old together or rip you open and harvest the heart. To me, it's simple, love or hatred, living with romance or killing with my bare hands."

She just looks at me.

"I like you. You are aesthetically appealing, both your face and body. But beyond fucking, we have better things to do, don't you agree?" I shed my coat and dress her up so as not to be distracted by her barely covered waist. "So? What's your name?"

"With all due respect, sir, you are one hell of a weirdo." Despite such mild humiliation, she pulls my coat over her back and forward, over her tender and pale shoulders. "My name is Beverly. What is it you want to ask?"

"Nice to meet you, Beverly. How long you have been here in Oscar's?"

"A bit more than two years, just after my graduation."

"Oh, really? I was told you are from Mistyhill but as far as I understand, there are only two high schools in that town, which one was it? Grammar school or Heritage?"

"Heritage, and then I left Mistyhill and went to UCRain."

"Ukraine?"

"No, UCRain. I meant my graduation from the medical school in the city, University of Central Rainbow."

"Oh, you went to medical school!?" I hide my surprise with all my might but clever as Beverly is, she catches me red-handed.

"Why are you surprised, Mr Atticus? A bitch can't be educated?"

"Sorry, I meant no offence but as you can see, you don't fit in the stereotype."

"Yeah, I was supposed to be a doctor, and look at me now." She avoids my eye contact, looking away, emitting endless shades of melancholy. There are no tears shedding but I hear an almost unnoticeable sniff generated from her cute little nose. Two years and a bit more time of body spoilage have made her less vulnerable but more pitiful. She was trained to save lives when at this point in this room she can't even save her own. I keep imagining that if I were not an asexual who came only for leads of my case but some dirty oily mid-aged pig, what would my reproductive organ do to the beauty of hers?

Her soft body is dressed in tempting lingerie and covered by my overcoat, which is reflecting the room's romantic light. It's so gentle that I forget the wave-particle dualism of light. For a second I think such pale warmth of her flawless skin is some sort of perfume, seducing my smelling sense and even my appetite. Partly under the bare concealment of her dark grey panties, I see a flower tattoo blooming on her left thigh, stretching up to her waistline and left lower back. The black ink isn't that intriguing but the slim curve the tattoo decorates is bewitching, along with the lace on her tiny top, slowly caressing her statuesque tall-standing breasts as she inhales and exhales.

And it hurts the softest place in my heart when I picture the way her customers so before they feast on her. Women are meant to be loved, not fucked. The ugliness and the wickedness of men's penises ruined the divinity and the gorgeousness of her body. Pushing in and pulling out, every thrust with which they commit their vandalism, is cutting to my soul. Every split second their filthy hands stay on her perfect skin is another torment to my mind.

An ancient Chinese poem once described the lotus flower as some holiness in the middle of the lake that 'can be only appreciated distantly but not touched blasphemously'. Aren't women the same? They are born divine, fair maidens from afar, and whoever dares to trespass with a boat to the heart of the lake to tarnish their majesty, will suffer eternally in the lowest circle in hell.

"What happened to you?" I ask to try to comfort her, yet my tone, though soft and light, sounds like some sort of confrontation. I am intrigued about what caused her miseries, and in turn, my heart's crying for her. My deep concerns for both Helen and the Osman family fade away at this moment. Right now, my soul will stay with dear Beverly. They say, he who saves a life, saves the world entire. If so, I'd like to redeem her innocence before me at this time.

"Just some failed love, no big deal." She smiles at me but she can't hide the depth of her pity and sorrow. Her pink lips slightly tilt upwards, trying to evade politely my intrusiveness, or rather, doubts of her own.

I sit next to her on the bed, with a certain distance between us. We both face the fire pit, as if in a therapy session.

"I had a friend from Mistyhill too," I say. "Once she was living happily with her loving parents, who had almost everything you can get in a small suburban county, fame and power. They'd kiss her young forehead every morning, they'd go out and bring back tasty dinner every day's sunset. Until one day, early in the morning, she woke up in complete darkness, and in her hands were the chill of the cold dead bodies of her parents. Beside her were those of more than 50 of her fellow villagers. She was surrounded by corpses of friends and their blood, which probably smelt unfamiliar to her senses from such an innocent childhood.

She was locked in that hell for three days until the odour of rotten flesh before finally being noticed. But the nightmare didn't end then. The police ended the case by claiming her parents' sin of mass suicide. In that underdeveloped small town, she was bullied intensively. Not a single day she wasn't reminded of her parentless existence and her born crime of being the devil's daughter. Not a single day she wasn't beaten by her 'peace-making' classmates or publicly cursed by the 'righteous' strangers on the streets. There was love for her until such short-lived love failed."

"Is she Helen?" she asks. "I used to know her. We were in the same class back in Heritage high school. Such a poor girl."

"So you knew her miseries, same old story, failed love." I sigh. "I accepted recently a case about her blackmailing a big figure in this city. She claimed that she had an original video of this man's son raping her. Regardless of the true nature of such a video, she is going to ruin a family. Are you planning to end up like her? Revenge for your failed love?"

I continue, "What you thought was failed love was just manipulative fate playing you as a puppet. You may have every reason to hate him but let him no longer hurt you and jeopardise your life. You still have a chance to rise again and withstand the cruel strong hurricane of destiny."

"I'm not a bitter avenger; I have no hatred against him. I…Perhaps still hold love for that man. But you can't magically bring him back anyway…"

"No, I can't, sorry. But you may still share your love stories with me."

"Will my storytelling bring him back? And the old days?"

"For a little while. For us. Storytelling is another kind of magic."

She prepares herself in absolute silence for a while. "I was in high school, and like any popular girl at that age, I had a boyfriend. He was the basketball star in the school team, six-two and handsome. I fell for him the minute I bumped into him making a three-pointer on the court. I remember crystal-clear that afternoon when he was shiny golden with sweat and his side-stepping technique producing loud but beautiful noise on the floor. That was my first love, and you know what they say about first love, every my subsequent affection on boys was in the mould of his specifications.

"We started to date soon after my innocent confession but before that, there were already rumours about my little feelings for him. I didn't tell anyone but the affections in my eyes had told all and triggered gossip. He said he liked me back, and I was in ecstasy. Therefore, every afternoon, I re-experienced the moment of *flipped* as my visit to the basketball court became routine. I'd bring chilled water for him in the hottest days of summer, and I'd walk him back to the dorm even in the coldest nights of winter. We were the prom king and queen, titled with 'the cutest couple'.

"Until his gambling father died, just like all those dramatic storylines of youthful farces, dumb and silly but also all kinds of catastrophic. He couldn't pay back his father's crushing debts but he said nothing to me. He chose to not drag me into this knee-deep mire of nightmares. Day after day, night after night, I started to notice bruises appearing on his slim, fit body, and sometimes even open wounds. New contusions, similar to hickeys, blossomed on his jawline. I mistakenly, like all girls madly in love, took the drug of jealousy and eventually had a fight with him because I thought he was cheating on me, despite his very trustworthiness to me. We broke up as the late revelation of such misunderstanding, my heart ached so much it was drowning in tears of my regrets and guilt. Sometimes over dinner alone or some early mornings while my head was still feeling fuzzy or when the bus runs over a speed bump, the sudden tiny weightlessness summons my memories. I long for the old days with him, and salty water just rains down on my cheeks. I missed him but I couldn't turn back time to tell him that I was sorry for my silly insecurities.

"He dropped out of school, and in haunting guilt, I went on to search for him all over town. I drove to his remaining relatives who had already given up on him, I asked every homeless person if they had seen him, and I even crossed the border between cities in search of him." She adds after a mild sob, "That's how I first came here and met Oscar, who offered me this job.

When I finally found him in a gutter, he was beaten half-dead. I held his weary arms and looked into his black eyes through the watery curtains in my eyes. I got him to the hospital. He told me that he still had to pay the debt of 10,000 euros. He yelled at me about the medical fees, asking me, 'Why did you bring me here?' He cried before me, which I had never seen him do. His bandaged palm covered his face but his agonising sobs told me all. He ripped off the IV and dashed towards my seat; he kneeled down and sank his head in my arms. 'Thank you. I love you.' He kept whispering these five words and kissed me at the end. That was the coldest kiss we ever had because his lips had restricted blood flow but somehow that's the best one also; my heart melted, and we kept kissing both in tears.

But apart from our reunion, we are still so much short in cash. The financial pressure suffocated us and that's when I decided to…" She pauses, turns her head in the shadows, and I can't see if she's shedding tears. "I had to. I drove to the city and came here to ask Oscar if he were still offering the job. He was, and I sold my first night for 5,000 euro. And ever after that, I just kept coming and taking clients. When I finally earned enough, I gave it to him without telling him where it came from. He didn't ask. I can recall the expression on his face, eyebrows pulled together and downwards to the extent that they almost joined his eyelashes, pale cheeks and weak arms showing he was still recovering from being near death. After dealing with the vicious creditor who charged a lot for interest, we finally came to embrace the peace and independence. At that evening, we used some remaining change to buy a bottle of fair wine to celebrate, dimmed light and romantic music in a cheap, tiny apartment, nothing to be compared with this fancy room but to us, it was a paradise. Until he found out my secret. We got slightly drunk, and we started to make out on the bed. He took off his shirt and my blouse; we embraced each other and showed ourselves to each other. He noticed a scratch on my inner thigh that might have been left by my last client. He got serious and questioned my integrity in the middle of a love-making, and I didn't know what to say to the man beloved by me. I was quiet but my silence only led him to fury. 'Don't lie to me, Beverly. What did you do? How did you get the money?' With all my unwillingness, I still spoke the truth, the ugly truth. I didn't dare to look him in the eyes but I could hear his dripping tears on the floor. We remained naked, while I sat on the bed and he stood before me. I tried to cover myself with bedsheets, yet when I looked down to grab them, he slapped me. 'Now you want to cover yourself? Why not then?' His palm hit my face as if we're pillow fighting. He was a basketball player. He could knock me unconscious with that enraged slap but he didn't. He started to sob and stepped back a bit. With my head turned by the slap, his penis entered my vision, which I had never seen. It was such an emotional and traumatising moment, the man I loved standing naked before me while his sexual organ was exposed clearly but the atmosphere was an apocalypse of embarrassment and my crushing guilt. I didn't know what to say or do, so I let the silent confrontation creeping on."

"Did he ever understand or forgive you?" I ask with compassion from the bottom of my heart.

"Yes and no. He packed my stuff and mailed it to my address in the city, not far from here. And he attached a letter. He didn't even say goodbye to me personally. In the letter, he said, he appreciated what I did for him but our relationship could not continue because of my wrongdoings. He said he could not accept a woman who sells her dignity and body to men. He said that though he still had deep feelings for me and wished me all well, such prostitution forbids him from making love with me, and therefore, there could be no love between us."

I stay mute, not daring to interrupt her silent crying.

"I read books about men's sexuality and all those stories about failed love and foul sex, hoping I can somehow learn to win him back. But I found nothing, what am I, Atticus? A bitch destined for foulness?"

I stare into the fire pit with a thousand shades of melancholy in my mind and finally speak. "Do you remember what we learned in school about Greek mythology?"

Her eyes closed, forbidding tears to overflow, and then she looked at me. "Yes?"

"Medusa was a fair maiden living happily in ancient Greece; she had the most gorgeous and bewitching long blond hair. Even the gods couldn't resist her beauty. She lived a joyful childhood and adolescence until she was brutally raped by Poseidon at Athena's temple. That was her virginity loss. She had no choice but lost her first night with a slutty god-man, not unlike your story. She was later cursed by Athena for her innocent 'crime' and became ugly, horrible and snake-haired. And that was her foulness. You see, maybe it's true, you're destined for such foulness, just like Medusa but that wasn't your fault. You lived on, sustaining yourself, regardless of what fate might torture your body and soul. And that's what matters."

"What happened to Medusa after being turned into a monster?"

That wasn't my point but I had to be honest. "Her unholy reputation as a murdering monstrosity had spread over the world, and finally, she was beheaded by Perseus and used as a weapon post-mortem."

I watch her shaking her head heavily as if trying to shake off the miseries and fate's torment. Her tears finally overflow, tarnishing her delicate makeup, the black eyeliners muddled around and her feather-like smooth hair stuck a little on her glowing cheeks. She whispers "no" repeatedly, like a madman selling insurance on the streets in a dumb show.

The Medusa metaphor is, perhaps, the last straw. She crumbles in on herself.

"That wasn't my point, dear. The point is, the poor girl Medusa did still live a life, despite all her pain and miseries. If she had managed to escape from that temple of god's filth that day, she'd have stayed a beautiful maiden but so what? She didn't have the chance to escape and therefore suffered her whole life. So what? To live a life, regardless of how fate's manipulation crushes you, is to find meaning in such a meaningless world. You can't fight the tyranny of your destiny, as we're mere mortals but you can rebel. You can stand still when the wind of fate blows hard; you can live a life with your own mentality intact and your own inner beauty shines.

Remember, to live is to suffer, to live on is to rebel, to live a life is to revel."

She keeps shaking her head but much less violently. Until it eventually stops. She stares right at me, eyes unfocused and pupils dilated. Her lips move with a string of saliva connecting them, trying to speak to me.

"You came for information about Helen. I can assure you, from nearly a decade of friendship with her in our childhood, she is not a person who will blackmail someone. If it were really the case, she meant otherwise. Worry no more about the video; she will never use it against your client if she had a copy at all."

Finally, I have what I need, and somehow her guarantee sounds promising and reliable, despite my little knowledge of the broken beauty before me. I grow, at this moment, careless for the farces all those people put me into, my excitement is easily overwhelmed by what comes after.

"And now?"

She takes off her lingerie, exposing her tender breasts, so very squishy and adorable. She opens up her long legs, showing the male-seducing penislessness in her crotch, the laces on her panties vaguely hide her vaginal flora and enhance its attractiveness. The look on her gorgeous face contradicts her seductive body language, so very painful and deeply hurt. She is trying to abandon her past and start anew. In a damn hard way. She had lost herself to grief and is recovering but at what price? Is the consciousness she regained the right one? I am deeply concerned, for that, I don't know. All I can tell is that she is evolving.

"Have funeral sex with me."

8

To fuck or not to fuck, the question lies before me.

I'm an asexual man, and I have barely felt, in my brief life, sexual arousal on three occasions: the art of whispering intimacy ASMR, the overly digitally manipulated animation of ahegao, which is the faces that chicks made in hentai showing an uncanny level of ecstasy, and finally, a woman's crotch. I wouldn't feel a thing, besides the aesthetic pleasure, watching strippers flashing their bodies three inches away from my nose but right now, before me, such an opposite of masculinity is pulling me closer, wanting me closer, needing me closer.

And at such close distance, I can smell the seductive feminine scent of hers vibrating from her thick thighs. Some scenes from *Scent of a Woman* resurface in my brain. I have an urge to drown my head between her thighs and embrace the holiness of her natural perfume. However, not just the law of 'opposites attract' applies on this occasion, not just the reptilian instincts activated in my functioning brain but also a voice in my head, more like a ray of moonlight, untarnished and divine, repel all thoughts of filthiness, telling me to just forget looking at her and to dance tango blindly and elegantly.

I stand up and move my feet, solo. I take a warm, wet towel hanging on the wall and hand it to her, while my footwork being smooth and tango dance-like.

She accepts my kind gesture and washes her face, wiping off ruined makeup to reveal her original and unadorned appearance. It's an even more lovable look, as if the makeup before, though 'formal' and delicate, were only to hide her gorgeous bareness from men's revelry of sexual hunting. Her eyes, after the mass production of tears, watery and pure, her naturally long eyelashes so curly that they touch her eyelids, bewitch me into some sort of foolish, reckless, blind love. Her raven pours down to her pale left shoulder, the right one bared by the turn of her head. Her lips, neither bloody red nor dim nude but in the shade of plain purity, the wrinkles and pink tinge blooming without the contamination of makeup.

I allow my vision to scan her bare body. She has nice smooth skin as her delicate breasts and flat tummy seem so stainless white and reflect the light like an image of ivory projected on a cinematic screen. Only her cute pink nipples, her belly button, and her slim curves decorate beautiful paleness. She pulls up her high-waisted panties, imprinting the shape of her outer vaginal labia on the thin cotton layer of her underwear. Or she doesn't do so; the mysteriousness of the scenario at her crotch is somehow so intriguing that I could write an investigative essay about it.

But her next move makes me forget about it. She removes her panties from between her two long, slim legs, exposing the most private part, the killer of men, the intimacy-seeking goal.

I don't get an erection. Instead, I curl my fingers, first slightly as the hiraken stance, then into a full raging fist. A few veins emerge on the back of my palm, and my knuckles whiten. I don't have much experience with women who intended to fuck me, or rather, I hadn't tried to pursue a sexual relationship with a human female since forever. But such an impact of this steamy sight only irritates me. Or rather, I feel nothing but the opposite of libido; her collarbones are so elegant that I want to rip them from her shoulders, her fat-free ivory arms subconsciously cover the breasts because of, perhaps, her last shade of shyness and shame, and I just wish to redirect the elbows outwards and tear them above her head, as if her arms will become her wings to reach the thousandth sky, her waist is so thin in a fabulous ratio with her hips. Such beauty is supposed to be crushed sideways so I can see blood pouring out from her cute belly button, or I should rinse it, make a few turns and see the creases spread over her whole abdomen. And after all, I'd love to saw off her legs, from ankles to upper thighs, just as trophies.

But I don't want to hurt her. Pain would be an unnecessary torment, and it would sour the atmosphere. Neither do I want to end her first. I hope to see her face, beset with facial expressions of peace and calmness, to watch me do these artworks with her body. Therefore, the muscle relaxants and painkillers would be merely two ingredients for anaesthesia. I need her awake to experience 'my sex'.

But not today. She's a poor girl with her lost virginity; she may still rebel against her fate. She can still live on.

I dress her with my overcoat again, softly take her face, and kiss her forehead, as gently as I ever possibly could.

"No, darling. I will not have funeral sex with you. You are fighting against your own conscience and your foul past. At this stage of spiritual nirvana, you are not yourself. I can see and I believe, tomorrow you'd walk out of the shadow of your 'failed love', and you'd be free. Working at what kind of job is your own business, I don't care, I don't mind but your true freedom will come from within. Live on, Beverly. As your name foretells, live on bravely."

She's lost in silence but shortly recovers her speech. "You refuse to have sex with me?"

"Sorry, I have…some issues. I'm mentally incapable of fucking."

"You don't enjoy the pleasure of flesh?"

"I do. But that's a different story. The extremity of intimacy…scares me. You see, I'm not far from broken myself. I can't bodily feel my love the way most men do, and I shall ultimately die alone on my abstinent deathbed. The comedy of *the forty-year-old virgin* turns into an epic tragedy on me, the most sacred human suffering fails to bloom for me as the deity of romance just walks away through me, as if I'm an immaterial ghost wandering around all this colourfulness while unable to exert influence on it."

For the very first time in a while, I dare to look at her in the eyes, a mutual torment brings us closer. I clear my throat, cutting our support-group conversation and start anew:

"You know, your opinion about Helen helps me a lot. Without concerns about the tape, we will know what to do next. Thank you."

"What are you gonna do?"

"There will be bloodshed, I'm afraid."

9

"Call this number and just say my name, the entire police special unit force will be under your command."

"Does that mean you found your answer?" asks Victoria.

"More or less. I guess an answer is no longer needed."

"Brilliant. Should I take that our rescue is justified by the legal system? You know, what about the tape?"

"Don't worry about the tape. There's a promisingly good chance she doesn't even have the original copy."

"So, when do we roll?"

"Now."

I put on my equipment, the vest, the radio, and all. This isn't my first time being involved in this sort of warfare but the discomforting tightness and barely bearable weight of my vest keeps teasing my sensible nerves as if I am a noob foot soldier walking into the battlefield of a suicide mission. My anxiety rises to the threshold of not noticing that a man has entered the room.

"Tori, I'm not letting you go without me. I'm going too. Count me in."

"Miss Osman? Who is this?" I turn to him.

"Atticus, this is my husband, Nicolas. Nicolas, Atticus."

"Nice to meet you, Nicola. We do indeed wish for more manpower but this war is no joke. Reconsider if you value your life."

"Atticus, right? I value my wife more, and what am I, if I hesitate to act? You understand me as a loving man, no?"

He utters his words genuinely, though his words and wishes may not sound so extremely touching as those husbands on the silver screen have portrayed such bravery a million times. I don't argue because I'd do the same if I were in his wife-caring shoes. Therefore, I nod to approve his involvement in this invasion mission.

"In that case, Nicola, wear your vest. And don't hesitate to use deadly force; we're facing a cultish rabble who may not reason with us at all. The goal is to rescue your father-in-law. Collateral casualties are not in consideration as the police will allow it for my sake."

He takes his equipment while looking at me in a strange manner. "But we are still not going to shoot to kill, right? I mean, try our best not to purge everybody in town?"

I stare back at him, speechless. I may be a saint, genuinely caring and loving equally for all human beings (Especially for pretty women perhaps) with my unique sense of compassionate pity, and I'm willing to do almost anything for their welfare but sometimes when the bigger picture is considered, I can still be the sinner. "Yes, that."

"Nico, don't let your sentiments blind you. It's not a merciless colonisation conquest; we're avenging our family's basic rights to be alive," Victoria says, securing a handgun on her thigh.

"That too," I say, as I have lost my silver tongue. I don't feel kinder than other men when I adopt rescue cats and dogs and shelter them with unconditional love, I don't feel I'm a better man when I donate money and resources to some charitable organisations for orphans' education. More recently, the same nice feelings don't emerge as well when I sit down with Beverly and treat her as a caring friend instead of a prostitute. However, in return, I feel no wrong when I threaten people in horrible ways for clients' personal benefits, or when I act as an outlaw, evading the legal system's punishments with my connections in higher society. I shoot to kill mercilessly as if those innocents are just long pigs waiting to be slaughtered. I recognise myself as an amoral person, free of the shackles of modern socially accepted morality. To guide my behaviour, I only possess a strong sense of integrity, not pro-social or antisocial, just laws of my own.

"Let's go. We will meet the police force in Mistyhill. Atticus, you drive before me to lead the way."

We go in two cars. I worry that my absence might intensify the stress in the air of the other car. We're at war, after all. They seem to be nice people. Victoria is more determined, while Nicolas is more caring.

I grab my walkie-talkie and start my first round of checking in. "Hello, Victoria? Nicolas? Are you alright? We are on the highway now, it will take us two hours maximum to arrive Mistyhill if the road remains open. I hope the atmosphere there won't be too tense?"

"Believe…is the best for sure…" The radio responds with a digitally manipulated buzzing noise, accompanied by broken pieces of their conversation.

"Hello? Can you hear me?"

The radio functions better this time. Even though my voice can't reach them, it produces their voices more clearly. Fortunately, calm and casual, nothing so stressful. But unfortunately, a bit too much, "Your list of the best batman actors were unmanageable. At least cut Adam West, Val Kilmer, and George Clooney straight off the list!"

Are they seriously discussing batman actors?

"Adam West was the first and the most original. Even with the disgustingly ridiculous costume, he deserves a place in the list!" Victoria argued.

"Oh, what's next? Are you going to tell me Clooney's bat-nipples were attractive?"

"Why not? Sexy as hell, hot as lava!"

"I don't think you're serious about this ranking."

"Alright, I was joking. Ha, of course, the nipples were too much, even for me. But if you cut them off, I'll cut Kevin Conroy off too."

"Why? He was a legend! His version was the inspiration for an entire generation!"

"But that wasn't live-action. Can we just stick with films?"

"Fine. So Keaton, Bale and Affleck." Nicolas' voice goes defensive. "You sure no David Mazouz?"

"Fuck off. I don't know who that is."

"Fine. The batman portrayal of my first time ever was by Keaton, fancy suit and all, still decent in the eyes of today. But I'll go with Affleck for the first place. Did you see that training scene in BVS? The power, the agility, the stamina, maybe he looks fat in that suit but all that bulkiness was muscles piling up! Bale might be realistic but Affleck was the kickass out of all for sure!"

"You call Bale realistic? You don't see a man dressing up in clown costume running in the streets and blowing up buildings and killing mayors every day!"

If they keep being this relaxed when we arrive, I see a dead mayor in our future.

"Much more realistic than an alien invasion. You Irish people have such so double standards."

"And what's wrong with that? I'd vote for Bale. He is also unbelievably handsome, I mean, is he part Greek?"

"Probably, I'm not sure. You think Greeks are good-looking?"

"Yeah, Russian girls and Greek guys are extremely attractive."

"That I agree with."

"That's also the reason I don't like them," says Victoria.

"I can understand your jealous bitterness for beautiful women but why don't you like beautiful men?" Nicolas, asks all curious. "Because of your insecurities? Come on, you totally deserve any of those pretty boys."

"Not exactly due to insecurities."

"I love Russian ladies and their hotness but I would withdraw myself before them, as my puny insecure little feelings interfere. What are your reasons? For disliking Greek men."

"Well...They look nice, so I subconsciously assume their inner niceness. Like a halo effect. One feature of a person will bring up high expectations of all other features, and such syndrome of glorification on someone often backfires at the admirers, ends up hurting them. Do you remember my ex? The Italian douchebag? He cheated on me twice but every time I still fell for his lies coming out of his perfect teeth and gorgeous lips, because I kept imagining how he was nice and all just based on the good looking."

"I can relate, I guess. Disney Princesses and their perfect love stories tricked us all, we came, in our innocent youth, to believe that the beautiful is the kind and the good. That was so very silly and blind, yet every inexperienced youngster mistakes."

My introspection on this side of the radio knocks the door of my mind, I shamefully take the blame on my wrongdoings...how am I not just someone like that, falling inevitably and helplessly for every piece of beauty that enters my sight? Call me a good Samaritan but who am I if not just an anthomaniac?

On the other hand, can anyone stone me? Only if they are not like me? The society or rather human nature, favours beauty, to the point only fans account becomes a huge money-maker! A collection of mere digital pixels that forms a sight of some random erotic art, can be a mainstream lifestyle, and isn't this fact mind-blowing enough?

Nicolas continues, "Yeah, attraction needs time to balance. The more you spend time with a person, despite the whatever effect, you'll see eventually who he is and finally find a way to accept who he is. For example, I don't have a halo effect on you. I've known you since we were young, like, five years old? We grew up playing in the same muddle, and I used to see your butt cheeks as a daily routine. And…"

"Yes?"

"That might be the reason I have issues in the bedroom."

It's not at all polite to hear their bedroom talk but since they are not able to hear me saying, "I'm here," and such conversation interests me, I allow myself to be a curious naughty boy.

"Care to elaborate?" Victoria asks.

"I feel like I know you too well, and we are so close. We are more like brother and sister. Our emotional intimacy destroys my excitement and my wish of taking you to bed."

I turn off my radio, not because I'm afraid they might catch me red-handed but due to my courtesy of not trespassing into others' private lives.

However, my old habit resurfaces like an OCD episode. I can't help but psychoanalyse their little sexual difficulty.

Such described dichotomy between sex and love, love-making and closeness, was firstly addressed by the biggest weirdo and madman, Professor Freud: "Where they love, they have no desire, and where they desire, they cannot love." Like how a later analysis categorised such paradoxical puzzle 'Madonna-whore complex', or from the perspective of heterosexual females 'saint-brute complex'; you enjoy the intimate relationship with Madonna and you worship this beautiful shinny star as your beloved partner but you just can't fuck her like fucking a whore. For straight, sexually charged men, it's either sex or intimacy, and there's no third feeling in-between. According to Freud, such a conundrum originated from the familial bonds formed between us in childhood and our primary caregivers. And because this bond also comes with the forbidden taste of incest, the fact is that our dating patterns lead us to choose partners who resemble our familial figures (When we were young). We are forever lost in the companionship with our loved ones, knowing them, caring for them but not fucking them.

I can perfectly understand, though being an asexual, the logic of straight minds of puny homo sapiens; I can fuck her when we just met but how do I get hard before her while she is preparing my lunch box for work?

For some pleasure of mental exploration, I keep digging into my case. The sense of a certain level of intimacy fascinates me, yet, like straight guys, it also bothers me, as if a dish of a heavily boned freshwater fish. I'd love to feast on such delicacy but also am agitated by the irritation of picking bones. I ache for it. How could I not? Aching for the purest romance, the most genuine support from a lifelong trustworthy partner, and the adorable chemistry in daily trifles that keeps a healthy commitment on companionship. The goodnight kiss generates the gentlest friction on her lips, the splitting hug before going to work initiates her unbearable waiting for me to come back to the place we call "our home."

The conversation they had probably fit the best my idea of true love. In the tense atmosphere of going to the battlefield, they still chill out to chat about who the best batman actor was, the dumb debate and the silly opposition echoes in that cramped space in their car. And after that, an intellectual discussion followed by a wholesome talk about reaching a better relationship. What more could you ask for?

Their intimacy moves me and shakes me to my core. I am forced by my sentiments to picture the scenarios; when

Victoria joked about her interest in Clooney's costume, at what angle were her lips tilted? Did her nude lipstick mark her palm when she covered her laughing mouth like a well-mannered lady? Or when she complimented Greek men's beauty, did her pretty eyes glow a shade of basic human instinct of aesthetics, as if seeing a masterpiece artwork from the Hellenistic age? Or when she asked carefully about her husband's mental block of sleeping with her, did her eyebrows frown slightly? Showing deep genuine concern for the love of her life, which I now believe she will forever be there by his side and stay loyal to the, no matter sexual or not, loving commitment of gold?

I feel instantly guilty from my next strain of idea; what if Victoria were with me? My cheeks blush gradually as my bold and vicious thoughts evolve in a spiral. I might be amoral but my integrity shames me, in some cases, equally. She is not gorgeous like all those women I met at Oscar's and in the grand church of Mistyhill but the very closeness between her and her husband makes me fall into the bottomless pit of jealousy, which greatly glorifies her feminine attractiveness.

What a woman! My thirst for a soulmate degrades me into a sense of insatiable wanting to be near her and to be around her. If the reality bends under my wish and I put my feet in Nicolas' shoes, would I marry this woman? I mean, I'm into comic book characters like Batman, as well as the Irish drinking culture. We would be a pair sharing lots of interests in my fantasies. I might be braiding her hair every night after her shower, curling it every now and then, I might as well learn to cook, purchasing Irish liquor and some fancy spices from stores and spending hours in the kitchen for a late-night feast. I might also take her to some local Irish pubs, nowhere close to the money-stinking Oscar's but places filled with Hozier's songs, and we would dance on the tables as if no one's watching.

Yet my sanity quickly puts out such flame.

Like how it goes in James Blunt's song *You're Beautiful*: *The angel I saw on subway was with someone else, we shared a moment that will last till the end but it's time to face the truth. I'll never be with her.*

Haunted by the melancholy, my feet grow tired and relax on the gas pedal but it'll be alright. The bloody billboard appears in my sight and a few special force mini-panzers show up there at the end of the road. I approach slowly and see around a dozen of heavily armed soldiers dispersed and preparing their weapons.

The war is about to begin.

10

I had thoroughly prepared myself for the bloody sight I had seen hanging on the billboard, yet the newly renovated billboard makes me experience once again the feeling of vomiting stomach acid.

The dead sheep were removed; a human male corpse has replaced them, the naked body covered by blood, not yet fully dried, and the limbless torso gutted like those lambs. The heavily armed soldiers stare at each other, being all at sea and not daring to look up. I share their fear, so does the loving couple behind me, Victoria even bursts into screams. Yet in the spirit of professionalism, I have to examine the situation.

His eyes, or rather, its eyes are wide open, speaking to me a touch of unbelievable surprise, as if Caesar in his last moment is whispering, "You too, Brutus?" Its nude torso is bulky and nicely tanned; nothing of it resembled the likes of an old man. The victim, though I can't see clearly at this distance, isn't Osman the mayor-to-be. So, who is he? I climb on my vehicle and try to examine such bloodiness more carefully. Its legs were sawed off at the level of upper thighs, and this man was brutally castrated, leaving a horrible mess in his crotch. Beside it, one word was written in blood, "Cheater." I stare at its seemingly familiar face that its features crushed altogether in horror, and a thunderbolt of realisation strikes me; it's Helen's boyfriend, Andreas, the one who kidnapped Osman before me!

Why is he dead? Was he cheating on Helen? Did she murder him? Who was he cheating with? Endless questions bombard my mind, and plausible answers are too many to be ruled out quickly. I brainstorm every possibility and ponder over the death's probable effect on this warfare that is about to begin. I feel hard to breathe.

Then I see another bloody object lying in the bushes beside the highway.

My heart stops for a second, previous difficulty in breathing transformed into a few seconds of suffocation, as if the air at the entrance of Mistyhill has been instantly sucked away, leaving merely dense mist caging us down. The special forces soldiers look along with my turned head and see the other motionless horror in the bushes. It's a dead woman with a huge open wound at her chest, the ribcage mercilessly torn apart, exposing the still heart and lungs. The breasts, no longer firm but dead stiff, are tarnished by half-dry blood stains near the edge of the horrifying wound. Her arms are intact and softly placed on each side of her torso, powerlessly laid in the lower branches of the nameless wild plants around her inelegant death. Her long legs are attached to her torso, thankfully, but their original beauty was barbarically taken as knife punctures mark on every inch of her legs' tender skin. She used to be young and beautiful, but now she died without any dignity, mutilated and just thrown away like some worthless garbage.

She's Beverly.

A thousand shades of raging fury and another thousand shades of regretful pity storm in my already nauseated head which can't be alleviated by any dose of aspirin. I don't care about the man's death hanging on the 'Welcome to Mistyhill' sign, but the humiliating end for Beverly is completely unacceptable. No matter what she did, regardless of whether she was innocent, she absolutely deserved no such bitter end. Moreover, she had been saved from her miseries just yesterday. A promising tomorrow awaited, but none of the meaningful essences in her life will bloom in my proud vision.

I suppress my anger and frustration with all my might, yet, while I pick her body up to the vehicle for a proper burial, my hands can't stop shaking damn hard like a Parkinson's sufferer. I'm going to get payback from whoever did this.

We march forward to the grand church with full speed and unstoppable rage. The secret invasion is successful. The building is surrounded quickly, and vanguards storm in, catching them right in the act of some sort of cultish ritual. The couple stays outside to block exists, and I, as the one leading the whole operation, follow the vanguards to enter. The cultists are totally surprised, and most of them are detained immediately. Some flee and are caught by backdoor sentries, some pick up guns, trying to fight back and are shortly taken down. Bloodshed was expected, but in reality, casualties are unexpectedly low. Three of the gang members are shot, including the big bulky one who previously took me down, two bullets go through his abdomen, and he soon collapses in the pool of his blood. I step on his upper body on the floor to enjoy my guilty pleasure while looking for Helen. Instead, a familiar face appears. The young monk who'd had a heated argumentative conversation with me is detained by a soldier.

I approach him, demanding, "Where the hell is Helen?"

"Fuck you."

I punch in his mouth, where his silver tongue lives. "Try again."

"It's too late!" He laughs out loud. "The moment you stormed in, she saw you all! She is, right now, probably slicing through his throat!"

I hesitate not at all, dashing to the entrance of the dungeon.

"We won the war! Hail absentees!"

I light up a flashlight and jump into the pit where my recent nightmares came from.

It was dark as usual but with the aid of my flashlight, I could barely see the rotten bodies and bones piling up on the floor. What I experienced by my touching was experienced again by my vision, my imagination had been pictured and the horror doubled, the only thing that stayed equally horrible was the smell, pungent and nose-piercing. It was a rather large basement, as now I could see, and at a corner, I saw one moving object.

With my compromised vision in this darkness, I see Helen is there covered in fresh blood, so fresh that it's sliding down her arms. Next to her lies Osman's body, motionless. Like what the young monk predicted, his throat has been cut deeply.

He's very dead, our mission has failed but my job is not yet done. I grab my karambit and dash to Helen, putting the blades on her throat. "Why did you kill Beverly? Why?"

The flashlight in my other hand is pointing at her face. With this close distance, I can see every drop of Osman's blood on her rosy cheeks. The bitch is still smiling! Her breath-taking beauty had been totally ignored in my aesthetics-seeking eyes. Fury fuels my almost harming a woman.

"I know you had your reasons for killing Osman. You were ruined by him or whatever, but why Beverly?" I yell at her.

"Oh, no reason." She smirks, showing her perfect teeth. "I found out my boyfriend, Andreas, was cheating on me with that bitch. What else was I supposed to do?"

"It's your man's fault. She probably didn't know your relationship with him! You knew Beverly. You were friends, right? How could you?!"

"Perhaps, you are right, but I wasn't thinking." Her eyes don't pass through any regret or sorrow. "I just killed. It's my retribution for them."

What a monster! A man as cold-blooded as I wouldn't even kill without hesitation, but a girl like her butchered two, one of them she had even invested feelings in, extremely mercilessly.

I should, if I abide by my integrity, remove her from this world permanently right now, despite all my chivalry. I reach forward with my hand holding the karambit to her neck, opening a slight cut, draining a little blood. Her face frowns as pain impacts her, but she does not resist or even scream, just enjoying the arrival of her death. She spends a second to fight back fear, as I can tell in her eyes, which she then closes and prepares well for the end. She doesn't shed a single tear, not even one drop of moisture spills from her closed eyelids.

Her gorgeous face heading up towards me exposes her vulnerable neck to my blade. I can see every flawless feature of hers embracing this moment, nostrils inhaling and exhaling peacefully as if she is standing before the calm sea and enjoying the salty freshness in the air, lips resting, its bewitchingly beautiful colour of scarlet shamed all shades of lipsticks, its dramatically sexy texture of firmness and smoothness out-valued all sorts of lip balms.

I give up on killing her. I give up on avenging Beverly, despite all my furious hatred for this heartless monstrosity before me. I drop my blade and step back, staring at her again with the help of my powerful flashlight.

She's in some casual clothes, relaxed but not plain, revealing but not so daring; an oversized high-cut thinly knitted sweater hides her tender breasts, but not her slim waistline, a pair of ripped jeans tightly fit her kneeling legs. Osman's blood had been spilt on her top but its decoration sexualised it in a fancy sense, the cotton has absorbed the liquid to make a new fashion.

She opens her eyes, looking confused. She is disappointed, brushing her hair with a bloody hand. But unexpectedly, this slight movement made her front hair fall down, becoming a cute thick bang.

Just like Lizzie.

As if I went back to that farm, the scorching sunlight in midsummer dims under the shades of the farmhouse, the piglets woo-weed all the way around us, a boy and a girl. The boy used to prank her daily for her attention. Well, he was a boy. And the girl happily enjoyed his harmless pranks. Well, he thought so. They had joy, they had fun, they had seasons in the sun, like two puppies woofing at each other and wrestling all the time, or two kittens licking each others' furs and napping cuddly.

I can't process any thoughts or ideas. Like a mindless zombie who isn't in control of any movement, I sprint towards her, lean over and kiss her on her scarlet lips. She is surprised, so am I, for my incomprehensible behaviour. I then hit the back of her head, knocking her out. She loses consciousness, fainting to her left, collapsing on Osman's body, as if, if you overlooked the splashing blood on their bodies, a loving father and a caring daughter were cuddling together for a beauty nap. Her face looks relaxed and peaceful, like an angel resting in utopia.

Thus, I am once again back to this hellish dungeon by myself, accompanied by a corpse and a sleeping beauty, standing straight and all so very alone.

11

It has been two weeks since the invasion.

And I'm sitting in my spot at Oscar's, drinking golden juice of hops. Its refreshingly chill foam washes from my mouth down to my stomach. Clark Oscar joins me in the silent drinking game. He has some whiskey in his palm. Its transparency allows him to see the neon disco lights flashing in patterns in his nightclub as he drinks.

We aren't talking, though we can. Oscar's new activity offers these coming joy-seekers special headphones for music and only plays it in their headphones. What a brilliant idea. I can finally drink in peace, instead of nauseating dizziness. The dancing, stepping noise and their hysterical laughter still ring out, but it's so much better than the crushingly loud music.

I, for sure, am not wearing headphones; the weight for me is not less annoying than its functioning. Neither is Oscar. He seems happy, no need for any catalyst for ecstasy.

"Did you find the tape?"

"Does it matter? The boy's life goes back to normal and will be in the future. Graduate from university, get a job, marry a woman. With the money his father left for him, he's lucky enough.

"The daughter?"

"She went back to Ireland with her husband. I heard she established a book editing company; the couple is running it smoothly."

"What happened to Helen after I gave her to you?"

"She's...you don't need to know."

"I'd like to know."

"Alright, since you helped me to overthrow Osman from the position, I'll be honest. It was a swift death; she didn't suffer."

"...Thank you, Mr Mayor."

"No, thank you, Mr Atticus. Without your help, Osman's ass would be in this mayoral seat."

I don't wish to reply. Instead of feedback, I take another heavy sip from my tall beer glass; the deliciousness overwhelms me into humility in my eyes.